ECHOES OF SILENCE

Dr. Raj Velamoor

TDW Productions & Publishing

Echoes of Silence
A Collection of Poems
By Dr. Raj Velamoor

First Published in 2025
Published by
TDW Productions and Publishing
New Delhi, India

ISBN: 978-93-91828-57-8

© 2025 Dr. Raj Velamoor
All rights reserved.

No part of this publication may be reproduced, stored in a retrieval system, or transmitted in any form or by any means—electronic, mechanical, photocopying, recording, or otherwise—without the prior written permission of the publisher, except in the case of brief quotations used in reviews, academic critique, or literary analysis.

For permissions, inquiries
TDW Productions and Publishing
Website: https://tdwpublishing.com/
Email: info@tdwpublishing.com

About the Cover
Inspired by the quiet beauty of reflection, the cover blends drifting leaves and gentle ripples to mirror the poems' themes of silence, memory, and emotional stillness.

Digital Artwork and Layout
The visual elements and layout features in this publication were digitally composed, edited, and enhanced using tools such as Photoshop, Canva, and Adobe InDesign.

Typesetting and Design
TDW Digital Graphics

Dedication

To my parents, who shaped my moral compass

To my wife, who walks beside me with grace

To my children and their spouses, for the love they give so generously

To my grandchildren, whose lives carry our story forward

To my siblings, with whom I share my roots

To my extended family, who nurture these roots in new soil

Each of you is a line in the poem of my life

Contents

Foreword – by Dr. Roopali Sircar Gaur   xiii
About the Author: Dr. Raj Velamoor   xv
Introduction   xix

SECTIONS AND POEMS

A: PULSE OF A NATION

1.	*A Paradise Lost?*	29
2.	*O Canada! We Stand on Guard for Thee*	32
3.	*Ode to an Outstanding Immigrant: An Appreciation*	36
4.	*2016: Dawn of a New Day?*	38
5.	*A Woe-men's Party?*	40
6.	*Joe and Jill*	41
7.	*The Line that Divides*	42
8.	*Echoes of Fallen Legends*	45

Contents

B: STERILE ROOMS & SILENT PRAYERS

9.	Don't Cry for Me Corona!	51
10.	Ode to IVIG!	54
11.	Mom in Surgery!	56
12.	Healing Grace: An Ode to Alison	58
13.	Trials of a Loved One Musings of a New Dawn	60

C: MILESTONES AND MOMENTS

14.	Ode to a Noble Lion	67
15.	Ode to a Life of Honour	70
16.	Ode to a Sister Beyond Compare!	73
17.	Ode to an Ailing Friend: A Caledonian Warrior	76
18.	On Turning 80: Ode to a Life Well Lived	79

Contents

19.	To a Companion: A Life Well Lived and Still Living	82
20.	A Roasty Toasty Ode to One Who Knows Too Much	88
21.	Ode to a Life Well Lived	92
22.	A Son Turns 40	97
23.	A Daughter-in-Law Turns 41 During Covid	101
24.	To a Brother – A Life of Benevolence	104
25.	To Polly with Love	106
26.	To a Sister-in-Law and Brother: A Golden Anniversary Ode	109
27.	A Daughter Turns 50	113
28.	A Son-in-Law Turns 50	116

Contents

D: EMPTY CHAIRS AT FULL TABLES

29.	Shradhanjali to a Fallen Brother: The Light You Left Behind	121
30.	Passing of a Gentle Soul	126
31.	Ode to One of a Kind	128
32.	Tribute to a True Original	131
33.	A Dear Colleague – In Memoriam	134

E: REARVIEW REVERIE

34.	Ode to the Medical School Class of 1964	141
35.	Ode to a Caring Friend!	146
36.	Ode to a Classmate: An Intrepid Spirit!	148
37.	Happy Mother's Day!	151
38.	A World Within Me?	152
39.	Ten Shades of Prose: The G10 Book Club	156

Contents

F: SERVING IN SILENCE

40.	Ode to Public Service – An Appreciation	163
41.	Ode to a Tireless Advocate – A Voice for the Voiceless	165

G: HOME IS A FEELING

42.	Personal Reflection If Truth be Told!	171
43	A Word of Thanks: To my Hometown	173
44.	Echoes of Generations: A Family Legacy	175
45.	The Cost of Desire: Emmanuel's Lament	177
46.	A Good Walk, After All!	179

Acknowledgements

With heartfelt gratitude to the friends who believed in these words long before I did.

To Dr. Roopali Sircar Gaur—

a distinguished poet and a generous spirit—thank you for your thoughtful guidance and for graciously opening the doors to the world of poetry. Your presence has been both an honour and a gift.

To my family—

your quiet encouragement lit the path of this brief poetic journey. For every word I found, you were the reason I kept searching.

To Dr. P. Koshy, Editor at TDW Publishing, and the entire team—

thank you for shaping this manuscript with such care and artistry. Your discerning eye and evident love for poetry have brought this work to life in ways I could only imagine.

Foreword

Echoes of Silence by Raj Velamoor is unique in its vocal acknowledgement of a life peopled with deep relationships and bonding. Each poem an ode to and a celebration of those who have enriched his life. Be it family, siblings, friends, colleagues and most importantly and poignantly the janma bhoomi and the karma bhoomi. India, the land of the poet's birth and Canada. the land that adopted him.

A psychiatrist by profession, a philosopher at heart and a magical wordsmith as a poet, Raj Velamoor's poems are dedications. Hidden within words of praise, he plumbs and presents the myriad facets of persona under poetic scrutiny. We do not miss the concerns and the resolutions. This is a book of poems that will be cherished by each member of his family and extended family. They will see the beacon of love and affection that a lighthouse called Raj Velamoor is beaming to guide.

In writing this foreward I have had the privileged opportunity of reading for the first time poems celebrating every connection. Lyrical and full of emotion for those of blood and those beyond blood, those present and those past, and those who will carry the future. There are in the silence between poetic lines echoes of bonds that helped find home in another soil. A conscious and subconscious memory of one's own roots and the new rooting through many routes. There is universal insight too, of lands and of people of politics and their far reaching consequences. The poet speaks of himself too, but shyly, and takes refuge in those who serve. His passion for golf appears briefly, as do his references to the medical profession, to survival in the pandemic while celebrating a birthday.

Raj Velamoor's words of dedication will remain deeply etched in the hearts of those who figure in this collection of poems. "Each of you is a line in the poem of my life."

Roopali Sircar Gaur, Ph.D

Prof. Dr Roopali Sircar Gaur, Ph.D. is a distinguished academic, poet-performer, novelist, and social justice advocate specializing in postcolonial feminist literary studies. Her seminal work, The Twice Colonised: Women in African Literature, explores colonial and patriarchal oppression, marking her as a leading feminist scholar in India. Retired from the University of Delhi, she also taught Creative Writing at IGNOU and has spoken internationally. She has edited over 30 literary anthologies and authored the novel Porridge and I: Growing Up with India. Founder-President of YUVATI and creator of Mera Kitab Ghar, she champions literacy and empowerment for underserved youth.

About the Author
Dr. Raj Velamoor

Dr. Velamoor's life is a mosaic of journeys, cultures, and callings. Born and raised in the vibrant city of Hyderabad, India, he set out in 1974 for England, where he trained in psychiatry and began shaping a lifelong devotion to understanding the human mind. Ten years later, he emigrated to Canada,

where he has lived and practiced for over four decades, eventually holding professorships at the Northern Ontario School of Medicine and Western University. He was a professor at Cornell University while working at the New York Presbyterian Hospital.

His professional path has crossed borders. He has practiced not only in Canada but also in the United States, New Zealand, and Bermuda, gathering layers of experience that continue to inform both his clinical insight and his creative expression. He has published over a hundred papers including book chapters in psychiatry that are frequently cited.

As a writer, Dr. Velamoor moves with equal ease between science and art. His debut novel, The Reunion (2021), tells the story of six friends from 1960s Hyderabad who, after decades of separation and migration, reunite in America to reckon with their pasts and present. The book received honorable mention at the London, New York, and Los Angeles Book Festivals, earning recognition for its emotional depth and narrative power.

Poetry, however, is where he turns inward. His verse is featured in the anthology Angst: Of Belonging and Not Belonging (2023), where he explores the themes of identity, exile, and human connection with nuance and sensitivity. His *poetic voice is informed by a life lived across continents, a life marked by constant becoming, questioning, and reflection.*

"I come from Hyderabad," he writes. "I studied in England, trained in psychiatry, lived in Canada, worked in the US. So many layers to who I am, and how I belong or don't. This is the soil my poetry grows from."

Now 79, Dr. Velamoor lives with his wife Suhasini in Toronto. His other home is New York where his children and grandchildren reside. When he's not writing or teaching, he enjoys the quiet discipline of golf, a game of patience, much like poetry and psychiatry.

Preface

"Poetry is when an emotion has found its thought and the thought has found words."

— Robert Frost

Poetry found me by accident a few years ago. It was unexpected, yet serendipitous. When my son turned forty, one of his close friends shared a limerick he had written for the occasion. It was just five lines. Short, witty, and full of life, with a rhythm that danced on the tongue. There was something light and joyful about it. That simple poem stirred something deep within me, and soon, I found myself writing my first poem, a sort of sonnet, shaped by the familiar rhyme and structure. Apparently Shakespeare loved sonnets which lends respectability to this genre of poetry.

Perhaps rhyme is the common man's doorway into poetry. It is welcoming, familiar, and full of music.

Free Verse on the other hand, the kind Walt Whitman wove into Leaves of Grass, or the soulful cadences of Tagore's Gitanjali, felt like a higher calling.

Tagore's Where the Mind is Without Fear is one such piece, so pure and so lyrical. The feeling of nationhood moves you to tears. It belongs to the realm of poetic nobility. I, however, find my place among simpler and common folk, the peasantry if you like, drawn to the comfort of rhyme, rhythm, and plain spoken feeling.

They say that, like people, words seek good company as well. Poetry teaches you to place each word in a sentence carefully and with care. This enables you to say more with less. I have come to love this quiet discipline of brevity and hope my poems spark a feeling in you.

In the beginning, I wrote as a gesture of love, small offerings for family and friends at their milestone celebrations of life. There is something timeless about a poem given as a gift; it stays with them quietly, long after the moment has passed. An incredible gift to give and receive.

Later, I found myself writing about the world beyond, about political changes, private losses, and hopes that flickered even in difficult times.

In many ways, writing has become a way of coping. A way to heal, and endure, during some difficult times.

Slowly, without quite meaning to, I have found myself with a collection! And encouraged by friends who believe these poems should be shared.

So here I am.

I hope these poems bring you a smile, a memory, or simply a quiet moment.

And more than anything, I hope they remind you, as they reminded me, that even the humblest words, when offered with love and honesty can illuminate the way forward.

Note from the Author

This collection brings together forty-five poems written over many years, some in solitude, others in gratitude, in grief, in wonder, or in reflection. These poems were not composed with the intention of publication. They began as personal expressions: to honour a friend or family member to mark a moment, to find clarity in confusion, or to capture what prose could not express.

The collection is arranged in seven thematic sections that mirror different phases and rhythms of life. The first, Pulse of a Nation, reflects my engagement with nationhood, public life, and political discourse, as both an immigrant and an observer. Sterile Rooms and Silent Prayers emerges from encounters with illness and healing, poems shaped by vulnerability and care. Milestones and Moments is the most personal of the sections, odes to family and friends across birthdays, anniversaries, and turning points. Empty Chairs at Full Tables remembers those who are no longer with us, holding their memory in tender reflection.

Rearview Reverie looks back on decades of friendships, nostalgia, and quiet joys. Serving in Silence is a tribute to those who give of themselves quietly, unsung public servants, advocates, and those whose lives are spent in the service of others. The final section, Home is a Feeling, returns to questions of identity and belonging, how we carry home within us, even as time and distance shift its shape.

While each poem stands alone, they also form a larger arc, one that begins in the public square and circles gently inward, toward memory, meaning, and the enduring presence of love.

A

Pulse of a Nation

1

A Paradise Lost ?

A country founded in 1776,
At Destiny's door with a jinx.
A shining city on the hill,
Stands to fall by its own will.

The Right and Left are at odds,
Pushing and pulling us daily apart.
A country it is of two nations,
Facing off like Siamese twins.

Adams, Jefferson and Mr Franklin,
Beckon you stand with your feet still.
Cherish the values that they epitomize,
And reject the currents that now divide.

A country concieved in bloody revolution,
Was poised to build a perfect union.
A house now divided within its walls,
Will fall if we defy the clarion call.

All are created equal was the credo,
And all lives matter was the motto.
This is no longer in the manifesto,
Of evil forces that promise to torpedo.

Lincoln signed the emancipation document,
And JFK roused a unified sentiment.
The ugly face of looming fascism,
Defaces the beauty of this divine coalition.

Framers of the mighty constitution,
Planted democracy in its bosom.
But migrant lives are in jeopardy,
And minority voices are now wispy.

Time now it is to wake from slumber,
And oppose forces that cast us asunder.
Choose we must the right side of history,
As the clock is ticking to seal our destiny.

Defining moment of a nation in strife,
Over two hundred years of celebrated life.
The moving finger will yet again write,
As the world holds its breath in prayer and fright.

Note: Written in November prior to the 2024 US elections.

2

O Canada!
We Stand on Guard for Thee

A country founded in eighteen sixty seven,
Our home of hope and glimpse of heaven.
A land of peace, so vast and free,
Iconic landscapes and wondrous Rockies.

Majestic mountains and rugged coastlines,
From Arctic tundra to lakes sublime.
Eagles trace the northern skies,
Through winter clouds and polar lights.

A tapestry of threads, woven in fusion,
Of immigrant stories and lives of inclusion.
Of myriad voices, joined as one,
A mosaic rich, of cultures spun.

Indigenous roots, proud and deep,
Legendary stories, the land vows to keep.
Wisdom passed through tryst and time,
Honored now and truth reconciled.

Springtime blooms with gentle grace,
Summer's warmth in nature's embrace.
Autumn's gold in crisp delight,
Winter's wonder, pure and white.

Confederation's hand guided the land,
Forging the dream of this Canadian brand.
Peacekeeping, not war, our proud decree,
Our sagely voice for all humanity.

ECHOES OF SILENCE

Beyond the world's storied border wide,
Neighbours in trade and dreams abide.
Bound by history, yet walking apart,
To carve our own destiny's path.

Tariffs raised, but unbent our will,
Tempers fray in this winter's chill.
Yet bridges stand where barriers will,
And friendship holds, through trial and chill.

From town to city, coast to coast,
Unity is what we value most.
Through rain or storm, we stand as one,
Together strong, whatever may come.

Oh, the 51st state, bless your heart!
We have heard that tale from the start.
No thanks, neighbour, happy with our lore,
And isn't 50 enough? No need for more!

O Canada!
We stand through calm and strain,
In sun, in snow, in wind, and rain.
True North, with hearts both strong and free,
We stand on guard for peace and thee.

3

Ode To An Outstanding Immigrant: *An Appreciation*

From Sri Lanka to Canada,
Receives Order of Canada.
A journey of citizenry,
And service extraordinary.

A journey of devotion,
And service to nation.
A journey of scholarship,
And inspiring leadership.

A journey to heal,
With commitment and zeal.
A journey of decency,
With grace and modesty.

A nation honors a son,
A life well lived and done.

4

2016: *Dawn of a New Day ?*

America has finally cast it's vote,
And Character it decided is important to uphold.

Dispelled it has the four years of darkness,
And rekindled the light of Hope and Saneness.

History will mark this as a sordid chapter,
Never to repeat come hell or high water.

Amnesty is due to the culpable by association,
And honour to those voicing righteous indignation.

A nation divided emerges from the ashes,
With a new president skilled in mending fences.

Empty Trumpty will not reincarnate again,
And spare this country from the ignominy of Shame.

A new dawn rings the liberty bell of freedom,
To echo the sweet chimes of 1776 in eternaldom.

5

A Woe-men's Party?

The Liar and the Lie
The only political ploy
For a party that will die
On the altar of its Lie
The only Man to hire
To save from the pyre
Is Liz Cheney on the fly
As a pie in the sky!

6

Joe and Jill

Joe and Jill
Went up the Hill
To administer and heal
The Evil Clown
And his base crying foul
Will don the orange gown ?

7

The Line that Divides

Bharat and Pakistan, born of one land,
Torn apart by a hasty hand.
Brothers once in soil and lore,
Split by blood in '47's roar.

One chose faith as its guiding star,
The other let many voices spar.
In one, the general's word holds sway,
In the other, the ballot charts the way.

One moves ahead with steady grace,
The other struggles to find its place.
One hears the hum of peaceful days,
The other walks through war's dark haze.

From shared roots and kindred flame,
They turned to rivals, none to blame.
A mirror cracked from east to west,
Each claims they have the truer quest.

The founders dreamed with hearts sincere,
Yet now, it's hatred we most hear.
Like Kurukshetra's fated fight,
They charge again in blinding spite.

Born of one womb, now worlds apart,
Two tales unfold from the same start.
Is it karma that drew this line,
Or hands that shaped their own design.

And Gandhi's warning haunts the air,
"An eye for eye" leads to despair.
Blind and broken, we'll both fall,
Unless we rise above it all.

8

Echoes of Fallen Legends

The twenty first dawns with promise thin,
As chaos brews beneath the din.
In eastern lands, the cannons roar,
While western hearts are split at core.

Economies crack, the markets strain,
Tariffs bite and fuel the pain.
The ships drift wide, no helm in hand,
No steady guide, no promised land.

Where are the leaders, brave and wise?
No Gandhi, No Mandela, no truth that flies.
They come, they go, they fade, they fall,
Footnotes etched, but none stand tall.

Few the footprints on our sands,
No dreamers left with outstretched hands.
No vision vast to light the way,
Just fleeting words that fade with day.

How shall we last through storm and tide,
This maelstrom time we cannot bide.
Will dawn arrive, or dusk descend?
We may not live to see the end.

Yet when all hope seems lost afar,
There rises supreme a bold avatar.
Through cloud and flame His clarion cry,
Will lift us up as he rides the sky.

B

Sterile Rooms and Silent Prayers

9

Don't Cry for Me Corona !

Maybe now a time to pause,
To make some sense of its cause.
While theories about the virus abound,
No one is sure why it is around.

Among millions to have sadly fallen,
Are health care workers who have risen.
Rank or station seem not to matter,
As princes and paupers seem both to falter.

For departed victims our hearts do bleed,
As their loved ones cry and grieve.
While we struggle with why now why this,
May their souls all Rest In Peace.

Fact of this is stranger than fiction,
To give us pause for some reflection.
Just when we thought we were invincible,
Corona warned "No you are dispensable"!

Unless we overcome hatred and intolerance,
Civilized we are not by any precedence.
Hunger and Poverty are still at large,
As equality between us is still but a mirage.

Swim like a fish we can for sure,
And fly like a bird we know to how.
But cheerfully forgotten have we not all ?
That being human is more important than all.

The only question that still but remains,
Will we learn a lesson from the remains ?
One lesson that Corona has taught us all,
That Humility we need to learn above all !

A fall from grace it has taken us all,
That we are creatures not great but small.
When we rise from this again,
Hope we look in before looking out again.

10

Ode to IVIG!

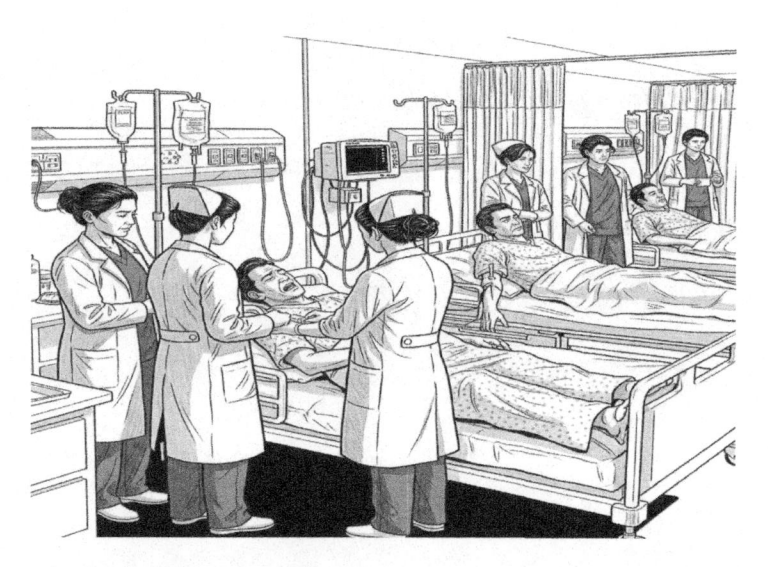

At the infirmary again,
For another infusion of same.

White coats and greens remain,
The colours of comfort and pain.

While Nightingales target the veins,
The legatees bellow with pain.

The drip drip delivers the flame,
To light up the cells lying lame.

While carers look up for solace,
The dear ones fight on for justice.

The flame will course through the frame,
And light up the alleys of her domain.

And tomorrow is a new dawn of fame,
As the sun takes over from the flame.

11

Mom in Surgery!

With the crack of April's dawn,
Day began at 4 with a sleepy yawn.
Mom, all nerves with prayers to spare,
Hopped in an Uber like she hadn't a care.

The hospital buzzed like a chaotic bazaar,
Registration felt like bidding on a used car.
Mom got her wristband, snug and tight,
And vanished into that surgical night.

I sat in the waiting room, hands in a fold,
Chewing my nails like they were made of gold.
Mom, knocked out in ether grace,
While I wore worry across my face.

Tick tock goes time, sharp and slow,
The surgeon twirls in a scalpel show.
And I wonder what dreams are in Mom's mind,
Mahjong? Book club? Grandkids in kind.

Tick tock goes time, each minute a grind,
While scalpels waltz, nerves intertwined.
And Mom, adrift in a chemical mist,
Dreaming of musicals she might've missed.

Now back she comes to hazy reality,
Post op fog and surgical finality.
Should I toast the scalpel's artful slice,
Or question this gamble with life's dice?

A day in the life of a surgeon,
And another in the life of a patient.
Will the two run parallel at odds,
Or intersect in common cause ?

12

Healing Grace
An Ode to Alison

For neck pain I went, a little dismayed,
To a physio's care, my fears allayed.
With cautious heart and guarded tread,
Unsure of what might lie ahead.

Then came Alison, with calm and grace,
Her soothing smile lit up my face.
She gauged my neck with hands so wise,
And saw the strain through knowing eyes.

Her healing hands began their art,
Unwinding knots and easing heart.
With every touch, the pain would flee,
And strength returned bit by bit to me.

She tuned her care to how I fared,
Adjusting gently, always prepared.
But what struck deep beyond the rest,
Was how her calm inspired the best.

A teacher, too, with wisdom wide,
She shaped Khushbu with patient pride.
If trees are judged by what they bear,
Then Khushbu blooms with skill and care.

In hands like these, health care finds its way,
With hearts that heal and minds that stay.
Grateful I am our paths did cross,
In this world of doubt and chance.

13

Trials of a Loved One Musings of a New Dawn

The year gone by
Not one of undiluted joy
It supplanted the course of life
Into a detour of stress and strife

There was trial and tribulation
And for our dear one suffering
At times it was close
But she rode out with force

Adversity she faced with grace
Bore pain with a brave face
She has been an inspiration
In our moments of desperation

We have to reset our roles
To suit her needs and goals
We have to recast our dreams
To align with destiny's new scheme

There will be hope and dismay
Maybe bumps along the way
While we gather the roses
Mind we will the prickly edges

There will be ups and downs
Like the sunrise and sundowns
As every cloud has a silver lining
Hope there will be to keep us moving

The new year will bring new openings
To the awful year thats closing
While Life is full of endings
There will also be new beginnings

The woods are lovely dark and deep
Have promises to keep before I sleep
Pledge we will to secure the storm door
From letting the squall back into our Home.

C

Milestones and Moments

14

Ode to a Noble Lion

He turns ninety today
With God's grace lighting the way.
A life of love and service,
Truth and honor in his practice.

He is a lion from Punjab,
Dignified and stately as a Nawab.
Guided by the tenets of Guru Granth Sahib,
Alongside his Begum, his adoring Mem Sahib !

He is a stately lion, steadfast and true,
Dignified in all he'll do.
Guided by the tenets of faith and grace,
With a loving partner by his embrace.

His words are measured, calm and wise,
His kindness shines in countless ties.
Never one to wound anyone or slight,
Princely in manners, just and right.

A gentle soul, both kind and true,
His warmth shines from his actions through.
With kindness wrapped in every tone,
He makes all hearts feel less alone.

A scholar's mind, a teacher's heart,
Taught school with distinction, a sacred art.
Following his faith with solemn pride,
Embraced truths that he abides by.

Proud father, friend and citizen true,
A guiding star in the skies so blue.
Has lived a life of meaning and purpose,
By being our society's moral compass.

His love stands firm, steady and bright,
Through ups and downs, through day and night.
Their marriage is an institution,
Of mutual love in pure profusion.

Their legacy shall long endure,
Through children strong and values pure.
Built on toil, love, and grace,
A family strong in time and place.

When all is said and all is done,
In this great lottery, we've surely won.
Fortune smiled and our paths did cross,
In this life of qualm and chance.

And so today, we wish him health,
Wish him peace and wish him wealth,
And we wish him happiness galore,
Finally Heaven, what could we wish more!

15

Ode to a Life of Honour

Born on Christmas Day,

And eighty-five years old you are today.

Blessed we are to celebrate this day,

To mark a milestone of distinction today.

A life of giving that began so long,
So much to so many for so very long.
Lives like yours are ones to cherish,
Labours of love and generous with flourish.

All notes in your family are now in harmony,
A grand piano it is of ivory and ebony.
With children, grandchildren, and loved ones near,
The music we hear is sweet and clear.

A Festival Day it is your birthday,
With deeds in spades over eight decades.
If immortality we through character gain,
Assured you are of this without fail.

We are proud of you with no end,
And thank you so for being our Godsend.
Yours is a life that's very well lived,
And ours especially by yours enriched.

Today you are young, just older than eighty,
A signal simply of second childhood officially.
Toys, treats, and tantrums, go all for it,
As surely by now, you have more than earned it!

The only area of improvement there may be,
Is to change your image of "brainy nerdy."
A "hole in one" to top off your CV,
Would round off your career to look sporty.

When all is said and all is done,
In this great lottery, we have certainly all won.
You have the love of friends and family,
And of the ONE above who keeps the tally.

We wish you and yours the best of health,
Peace of mind, with all dues dealt.
Family love and happiness galore,
And finally Heaven, what could we wish more?

16

Ode to a Sister Beyond Compare!

The only daughter in the family,
Gentle in nature with grace and dignity.
Today we celebrate your turning seventy,
Even if we are not in close proximity.

Born you were on August the fifteenth,
When India with destiny made its tryst.
A family welcomed this daughter's arrival,
While a nation celebrated with pomp and carnival.

Though lost in the crowded family shuffle,
Poise was kept with no sign of ruffle.
While others their views express garishly,
Assert you have, your presence serenely.

Lucky we are, for the one you would marry,
A brother he is, to us in the family.
While calm you are, and cool as a lily,
Agile he is, as a Duracell battery.

All notes in your family, are now in synchrony,
With children and grands, in sweet harmony.
A grand piano it is, of ebony and ivory,
With all keys playing in sync and melody.

Dear Sister, you have aged so gracefully,
Softly speaking, polite and warmly.
Forgiving you are, of others' foibles,
Sweet by nature and untouched by trifles.

Living so plainly, but comporting elegantly,
Thinking so sagely, and acting so fairly.
You sing like an angel, with cadence and melody,
Making even life's prose, sound like poetry.

A life lived with manners and decency,
Despite many trials, in the journey to seventy.
Proud we are, of your life and family,
And grateful always, your kindness so warmly.

Oceans away may be, our distance physically,
Separated by miles, but not so, emotionally.
While missed you are, in our midst dearly,
But always remembered, in our thoughts fervently.

We wish today, the best of health,
Peace of mind and enough of wealth.
Wish we could share our times some more,
In the time that's left, for us evermore.

17

Ode to an Ailing Friend
A Caledonian Warrior

A man of vintage Scottish pride,
Polite and reserved, with wit inside.
Forthright and honest in his deeds,
Says what he means no hidden creeds.

Disagree he may with such ease,
But never does he with malice or tease.
Patriotic he is, his homeland's son,
Defends her honor with passion and fun.

A true citizen of lands anew,
Polished, kind, and genteel too.
A man of culture, taste refined,
With arts and music intertwined.

A natural hand in games of grace,
Golf and tennis his lively chase.
Has served his calling, true and fair,
With diligence and devoted care.

His patients hold him in esteem,
For kindness wrapped in every scheme.
Relishes a good pint, frothy and deep,
Even a dram of whiskey to keep.

Brave and bold he has been,
In battling the enemy within.
Tough and strong, he's faced the fight,
With spirit strong and will so bright.

A braveheart's fire, a leader's stand,
Dogged as history's steadfast hand.
Yours is a life well lived,
And ours by yours enriched.

When all is said and all is done,
The gift of your presence we have won.
We send our wishes, warm and clear,
This season of hope and prayer.

We hope to have you back next year,
For gracing our book club with literary flair,
God willing next year will be that year,
A Caledonian comeback as a true highlander.

18

On Turning 80
Ode to a Life Well Lived!

Born in Germany, rich in history,
A precious only child to the family.
To America came but on a whim,
And settled in Canada to live the dream.

In Toronto, met a love so true,
And in love, fell head over shoe.
A North Star to guide along the way,
Adrift they'd be without that day.

Together they raised a beautiful family,
A grand piano it looks, with ivory and ebony.
With all keys playing in tune and harmony,
The music we hear is sweet in melody.

Confidence grew as the years went by,
A huge success made in professional life.
A leader who helped many companies thrive,
Reshaping their fortunes to grow and shine.

Known in our book circle for quite some time,
Finance and business are his favourite kind.
With study and inquiry, precise and concise,
Each review thoughtful, measured, and wise.

But it's quite another story when it comes to golfing,
Not always on time, sometimes delaying.
While friends are swinging on the first tee,
Still arriving leisurely, taking it easy.

Today, turning a ripe old eighty,
A signal really of a second childhood officially.
Toys, treats, and tantrums, go all for it,
As surely now, have more than earned it.

Glad we are for this company,
A part we are of this life story.
Have no regrets of unfulfilled endings,
As life is yet full of rich new beginnings.

When all is said and all is done,
Love and respect have been won.
The journey that started far away,
Now a proud part of Canada today.

We now raise our glasses in celebration,
And make this toast in admiration:

For a long life and a healthy one,
To a good love and a cherished one.
Peaceful days ahead and exciting ones,
For a good drink and then another one!

Happy Birthday!

19

To a Companion
A Life Well Lived and Still Living

Born on the 23rd of July
In an Indian city under the sky,
As the last one to arrive,
Bringing her family joy and pride.

Carefree as a child,
With not a worry on the mind,
For company turned to dreams and stories,
In the make believe world of Aesop's fables.

From one city to another, family moved,
As childhood gave way to teenagehood.
Schooling was in a convent's embrace,
With nuns and mothers guiding the ways.

With friends so dear and always true,
Bonds of friendship only grew.
Adding warmth to beauty and charm,
A humane person would gently form.

Higher studies called upon to see,
If humanities would suit the mind's decree.
Math and science brought no delight,
But languages and arts took brilliant flight.

A graduate with a Bachelor of Arts,
Immersed in books of all sorts.
Journalism became the next pursuit,
A master's diploma now her suit.

In the midst of study and reflection,
A distraction loomed with a new connection.
Life's headaches would soon begin,
From a companion through thick and thin.

After much strife and family dissent,
Marriage arrived with tacit consent.
A bride soon tested with loss so strong,
Navigating life with mom now gone.

The family vessel set to sail,
Through gentle winds and mighty gales.
Love and care defined the way,
Even as grief refused to fade.

Books became an escape so sweet,
From foreign lands and unfamiliar street.
A new arrival brought fresh delight,
As life moved forward in steady flight.

Through duty's weight and love's demand,
Bearing burdens with a steady hand.
A move to Canada, a brand new start,
In a land so kind and warm of heart.

While raising children with love untold,
Another chapter would soon unfold.
Midnight oil at forty burned,
Another master's degree proudly earned.

The finest hour then arrived,
A career where she greatly thrived.
Refugees seeking a safer shore,
Found her kindness so much more.

Migrant faces joined, her family grew,
A loving home for all they knew.
Giving freely, answering calls,
Supporting lives both great and small.

Missing a beat or two with every loss,
Of loved ones gone yet never lost.
Still standing strong, despite the pain,
Giving and guiding, time and again.

A life of giving, long and true,
So much offered, much to do.
Labors of love without refrain,
A heart so full, without a stain.

A life to cherish, proud and bright,
A steady flame, a guiding light.
Not only with family's love embraced,
But by the one who keeps the trace.

Seventy years, a journey so grand,
With kindness dealt by steady hand.
If immortality is love's refrain,
It is assured, again and again.

Now the road ahead is clear,
A compass guiding, ever near.
A light that shines through every gloom,
A flower that through darkness blooms.

Wishing now the best of health,
Peace of mind, and all debts dealt.
Fables with tales of happiness galore,
And finally heaven, what could be more?

ECHOES OF SILENCE

20

A Roasty Toasty Ode to *One Who Knows Too Much*

Seventy seven comes today,
With body parts still in play.
Keeps both mind and frame in sway,
By huffing and puffing genially away.

There is nothing the matter with these wits,
Except perhaps for those curious myths.
Inside, a younger soul still lingers,
Wondering what happened to time's swift fingers.

The defining grace, without a doubt,
A partner chosen, the perfect route.
And roots set firm in a place so bright,
Full of culture and pure delight.

A pulse so strong, blood running thick,
And awfully fit despite the width.
Imagination racing, head in flight,
Yet astute for one of seasoned sight.

The morning starts in busy sway,
Plowing through cyberspace each day.
While others skim through what they see,
Reading between the lines comes naturally.

While many follow today's new ways,
A mind still roams in yesterday's days.
While dreams drift toward the western light,
Visions awaken in the east at night.

Boyish still, with endless pep,
Swinging a racket, taking a step.
Savoring life with zest and vigour,
Sizzling with piss and acid vinegar.

A mind admired evermore,
Though at the stairs, unsure.
Going up for something in hand,
Or just came down, forgot the plan.

A seeker of knowledge, far and wide,
With wisdom deep, yet hard to guide.
A learning curve that curves anew,
Though sometimes wanders in the blue.

Life is like that ten-speed ride,
Not using all the gears inside.
Yet climbing hills, both high and low,
Seldom faltering as they go.

The moral, as this tale unfolds,
We all are flawed as we grow old.
Better to grin and say, "All's fine,"
Than to reveal the state we're in!

Now raise your glasses to a timeless toast,
A wish for all, from coast to coast:

To a long life and a healthy one,
A good love and a steady one,
A quick passing and a painless one,
To a good drink and then another one!

Happy Birthday!
And may you live as long as you want!

21

Ode to a Life Well Lived

Eighty years have come today,
Weathering many a storm along the way.
We are here to celebrate this day,
And to wish for many more to stay.

Let us now look back on this life,
To get a measure of the ride.
It would not be a stretch to say,
That today should be Appreciation Day.

Once just an innocent little miss,
Until fate waltzed in, and things went amiss.
It would not be an exaggeration to say,
That luck struck big in the lottery that day.

A father once said, "Daughter, don't dread,
Look forward to the future ahead."
Promises of joy and fun were made,
But challenges also came her way.

Partnerships such as this are rare,
Few marriages can truly compare.
If matrimony had been swapped for another fate,
A pardon might have come of late.

A land of hope was chosen bright,
A new home built with love and might.
One carved a path of changing ways,
The other stood firm in steady days.

Children arrived, and the family grew,
A home of love, where dreams came true.
Support was given in all their strides,
And they excelled with joy and pride.

I often wonder how it was done,
With odds stacked high against the sun.
The simple answer, as I see,
Perhaps half was spent in peaceful sleep.

Eighty years may mark today,
But forty is all that may feel in sway.
A lesson here for all to take—
Being too busy is often a mistake.

Calm and peaceful through the storm,
A steady heart that beats so warm.
Moving gently, slow and sure,
Even hurricanes would wait their turn.

She walks and moves in measured grace,
Like astronauts drifting in open space.
Conversations flow, though with delight,
A pause may come before the night.

Though soft in voice and gentle in air,
A rock for all, always there.
The glue that held both joy and pain,
In sunshine bright and in the rain.

So much has been given for so long,
Now it's time for rest before too long.
A defining moment now is near,
To sit back and let love steer.

A partnership strong, a bond so tight,
A dance of patience, day and night.
If only to add some madness slight,
To make the journey feel just right.

A lesson here for those who see,
Longevity's secret may simply be—
A touch of prose, a bit of rhyme,
And love that stands the test of time.

When all is said and all is done,
A precious pearl, a life well-spun.
For kindness given, love so swift,
A heart so full, a lifelong gift.

Eighty years, how truly nifty!
With love that's never thrifty.
Special beyond words, ever daily,
If you dears catch my drifty!

22

A Son Turns 40

Born in Coventry, England,
In the UK county of West Midlands.
Arrive he would in unseemly hurry,
Mom barely making to the labor room flurry,
And dad not even present for the delivery.

As a child, he had an obsession,
An almost meticulous fixation.
Clothes were folded very very neatly,
And beds made crisp and wrinkle freely.

Halloween candy was hidden discreetly,
Baseball scores were tracked scrupulously.
Concerns arose, would he turn out crazy?
With such quirks, perhaps just maybe.

Shy and puny, withdrawn and nerdy,
Preferring the indoors over the sturdy.
Outside games held little sway,
As home was the preferred stay.

Tied to a mother's embrace so tight,
Separation would bring forth fright.
Nervous again, concerns arose,
Would this be a path that forever flows?

Friends were few, social circles small,
And interest in romance hardly at all.
Offers were made to arrange a date,
Yet each time, the answer was to wait.

Concerned inquiries were brushed aside,
With a firm request to step aside.
Tall he grew, lanky and lean,
A figure almost unseen.
Front to back, nearly the same,
A silhouette that barely remained.

Tennis was played with skill and might,
A resemblance to Pete Sampras in sight.
Yet the comparisons would halt right there,
As competition was never a thing to bear.

Serious trouble was rarely caused,
Unlike a sibling who often was.
But once, a car was taken for a ride,
Without a license to coincide.
This tale shall stay within these walls,
For secrecy's sake, lest trouble calls.

A degree in law was then attained,
With accolades earned and prizes gained.
A union was formed, a life was shared,
Bringing pride and love declared.

Children arrived, joy in tow,
Adding brightness to life's flow.
A relief to see them strong and bright,
And, thankfully, knowing how to swim right!

Jokes aside, the place is right,
Everything that matters shines so bright.
Looking back, the thought is clear,
Perhaps the concerns were misplaced in fear.

Forty years now, have been reached,
Yet youthfulness remains within reach.
A twinkle still gleams in the eyes,
A warmth that never ever dies.

As years add on and lines appear,
And silver strands replace the clear,
Why should there be a single care?
For the one who counts is up in the air.

Happy Birthday Son !

23

A Daughter in Law Turns 41 during Covid !

Let's raise our glasses on this day,
For planning this soirée on Zoom today.
Though we live in our bubbles today,
Here's a shout-out for a birthday today.

A milestone reached, forty and one,
Without much fuss and little fun.
None before or after matches this day,
As stranger than fiction this birthday is today.

Though separated by social distance,
Love bridges the physical distance.
Hugs are sent through virtual space,
Defying the forces that rig our place.

Gifts we would, but can't send any,
Boxed or not, not even money.
Ice cream cake shall have to wait,
Blow candles though, we can participate.

As curls are grabbed and twirled,
This may bring some cheer for mirth.
Through these days of idle and gloom,
The birth star shines for better days to loom.

On this 41st, a new day dawns,
And hope rises as tides turn strong.
With changing winds, there's hope anew,
For brighter days and skies of blue.

Challenges may come and challenges may go,
But fortune and joy will continue to grow.
With love and laughter filling the air,
A gift of family beyond compare.

Here's to a good life, a healthy long one,
A beautiful partner, and a thoughtful one.
A good career, and a meaningful one,
A good drink and then another one!

Cheers!

24

To a Brother
A Life of Benevolence

We celebrate your birthday today,
As you turn eighty in a special way.
Kind and gentle, you've always been,
With words well-measured, thoughtful, and keen.

You have fulfilled your roles with grace,
A devoted husband, brother, and father to embrace.
You've served your community with heart and skill,
Earning a reputation that shines through still.

There is much to learn from you,
In handling life's trials with wisdom true.
A silken touch, so rare to find,
In a world often harsh and unkind.

If we reflect upon your years,
Your journey stands tall, inspiring and clear.
A life well lived in every way,
A soul to honor, a light to display.

May you have many more years to hold,
Guiding us as the family's stronghold.
Take good care as time does unfold,
For you are cherished and precious as gold.

25

To Polly with Love

It's your birthday today
As another year has passed this day
A special person you are to us
As so much joy you bring to us

You are the child that was full of grace
Honest and truthful in your ways
And the child that was loving and giving
Living a life of purpose and meaning

You say what you mean
No bell there is to unring
And mean what you say
No page there is to rephrase

It's time to party and yes celebrate
And embrace the changes that come with age
Count not the candles on your cake
As your charm surely defies your age

You are blessed with lovely children
And their spouses and grandchildren
Gorgeous your family is like a grand piano
Notes all in sync like a sweet concerto

We take this moment to thank you so
For all the things you do and more
May you gain more than you give
As its time for you to receive

We sing happy birthday to you and cheer
As we think you are such a dear
May you live as long as you wish
As by you Prolly our lives also enrich

We wish you health and wish you wealth
Family love and happiness copious
And finally Heaven we wish for you
Where you belong just for being YOU !

Happy Birthday !

26

To a Sister in Law and Brother
A Golden Anniversary Ode

Most marriages begin as poetry,
And live out in prose through history.
To honor this golden celebration,
We revisit a love's foundation.

Half a century ago, they say,
A wonderful journey began this day.
Two souls united, side by side,
With love and trust as their guide.

He had a vision, a plan in mind,
For a partner graceful and kind.
Her father said, "No need to fear,"
For a bright future was drawing near.

Love and devotion were promised then,
A bond unshaken through thick and thin.
Yet surprises came along the way,
For life has a script none can portray.

"You have the loveliest eyes," he said,
With laughter and blushes widely spread.
"Tell me more," she coyly replied,
As love and reason walked side by side.

Through years of joy, through trials too,
They built a life so strong and true.
A family flourished, love grew vast,
Rooted in memories that will always last.

Not always singing the same tune,
Yet finding harmony in sun and moon.
Through changing tides, through highs and lows,
A steady love forever flows.

You are a couple sociologists must study,
To know the secret of your longevity.
While unions these days are under siege,
Here we are celebrating your 50th anniversary.

Fifty years what a milestone grand,
A testament to love that stands.
With wisdom, patience, and a guiding light,
You've made the journey pure and bright.

Of years you have accumulated are 50,
We think that's really nifty.
With love you are never thrifty,
You are really special, if you catch my drifty.

So here's to you, a toast so true,
For love that only stronger grew.
Through time and trials, joy and fun,
In love's great journey, you have won.

27

A Daughter Turns 50

Hard to believe, yet here we are,
Our little girl has come so far.
Our firstborn child, so full of grace,
With kindness glowing on her face.

Gentle hearted, strong, yet so mild,
Forever generous, ever since a child.
She braved the storms youth often sends,
With quiet dignity, that softly mends.

Those early years brought trial and test,
But through it all, she gave her best.
With wisdom born of struggles deep,
She learned to cope, in word and deed.

She chose a path of healing needs,
Of people in pain and worries deep.
With humble hands and serene face,
She found her purpose, found her place.

She taught while serving, heart so kind,
A rising tide she could not hide.
A professor crowned in record time,
With poise that made the climb sublime.

Then NYU came knocking loud,
To honor her among their best and proud.
They saw the spark, the boundless light,
She brings to every student in sight.

To all she meets, she leaves her trace,
Of warmth, of wit, of quiet grace.
A force of love, of wisdom clear,
Her gentle magic draws all so near.

And now she stands at fifty bright,
With love and family held so tight.
We raise a toast with blessings sincere,
To fifty more, and glorious cheer!

You've aged like wine, refined and rare,
A soul beyond compare, joyful and fair.
So here's our wish, both proud and true,
Long life and mirth, we so honour you.

28

A Son in Law Turns 50

A man of simple, quiet grace,
Turns fifty no fuss, no frantic pace.
Gentle in manner and in face,
Measured in words, in step, in place.

Supportive of his wife's bright dreams,
Caring for his girls' esteem.
He walks with care, with depth of feeling,
Through life's highs and lows, revealing.

Morals and ethics of a saint,
Guide him gently, free of taint.
He serves his patients with quiet faith,
Earning their respect in spades.

Fifty now, with calm elegance,
He shows the way of benevolence.
A man of few words he may be,
But his character shines bright and free.

The next years of his journey unfold,
With our love and blessings told.
Health and joy we wish you more,
As you walk with grace as before.

Happy Birthday Son !

D

Empty Chairs at Full Tables

29

Shradhanjali to A Fallen Brother
The Light You Left Behind

On this summer's day, we gather in joy,
to celebrate such a vibrant life.
With solace we honor, not with tears,
a brother's journey, through the years.

In the family shadows, where memories lie,
we remember our brother, who touched our life.
With a heart full of merriment, a spirit so free,
he painted our lives, with his joyous spree.

On a September day, a life took flight,
born in the bosom of summer's light.
A child of the harvest, of ripening fields,
with dreams as vast as autumn yields.

Warm childhood days and crisp cool nights,
brought forth a soul with vivid sights.
With the balance of seasons, poised and fair,
a spirit of radiance, born beyond compare.

September's breath, in his laughter's sound,
as leaves turned amber and fell to the ground.
In each falling leaf, a story spun,
of an odyssey begun, not yet done.

His eyes held the stars, his smile the sun,
a journey with him was a race well run.
In the fields of our youth, he was the breeze,
the echo of laughter in the rustling trees.

In the realm of work, his star did rise,
with skill and grace, he reached the skies.
Many young lives he nurtured and groomed,
his legacy through them, sealed and secured.

His voice, a melody that soothed the soul,
each note a whisper, made the broken whole.
In songs, he weaved magic, pure and bright,
a gift of serenity, sounding just right.

In the winds of March, he took his leave,
leaving us forlorn, saddened to grieve.
A dear brother gifted, a heart so kind,
to hold in memory, in the depths of our mind.

A March day was bleak, yet ushered new life,
and took away a soul, ending mortal strife.
Blossoms bloom where he once stood tall,
his laughter now, an echo in the hall.

The March winds whisper his gentle name,
his love will endure, an eternal flame.
In each new dawn and starry night,
we feel his presence, pure and bright.

Gone too soon, like a whisper in the night,
leaving us longing in the dimming light.
Yet his essence lingers, in each tear and smile,
his love and laughter, spark memory's mile.

The rains of spring, they gently fall,
a tender reminder of his austere thrall.
His spirit like budding leaves, quietly calls,
that inner voice in us, that we often recall.

Those he adored, his family, his own,
with love, he shaped a life well known.
Gone, yet his love lives on, a guiding light,
their hearts he held dear, each day and night.

As seasons turn and time moves on,
his memory will remain, never ever gone.
A beloved's love, forever in our hearts,
Brother, rest now, the divine odyssey starts.

His voice is silent, but his spirit survives,
in the hallowed life of our family's memoir.
We'll hold him close, through sorrow and mirth,
our youngest brother, who brought heaven to earth.

The doors of heaven open, says Lord Krishna,
in the famous mantra of the Bhagavad Gita.
For warriors like him, who rejoice the dance,
to have such a battle thrust upon by chance.

30

Passing of a Gentle Soul

A life so refined, a presence so mild,
Softly spoken and sweetly smiled.
Words voiced with caution and care,
Carefully weighed and always fair.

A heart devoted, steadfast and true,
Placing duty above what was due.
Treating others like family near,
Giving love so sincere and clear.

A presence noble among all,
With praise and respect standing tall.
When all is said and all is done,
A legacy remains, a life well-spun.

Thoughts go out to loved ones dear,
As they hold each memory near.
Celebrating kindness, and humility,
A life well lived with grace and dignity.

Wishing peace on this final way,
A path of roses laid today.
Honoring a soul of decency,
May it rest in peace eternity.

31

Ode to
A One of a Kind

A force of nature, bold and free,
Lived life on her own decree.
Said what was meant, meant what was said,
A fearless spirit, far ahead.

Reveled in life's many thrills,
Fast cars, open roads, and rolling hills.
Fearless in passions, unafraid to dare,
A spirit so rare, beyond compare.

Words were sharp, wit astute,
In debates stood quite resolute.
Cherished a challenge, embraced the fight,
Defending views with all her might.

Beneath the strength lay a gentle heart,
Compassion and kindness played their part.
Listened with care, sought to understand,
A tender touch, a guiding hand.

Adversity came, as life often tests,
Met it head on, courage expressed.
Unyielding and bold, faced each strife,
Living with valor, her hallmark in life.

Will be remembered, steadfast and true,
A light that touched all it knew.
Even as time settles the dust of days,
A legacy endures in countless ways.

A soulmate, loyal and faithful,
In his heart, love forever renews.
Eternity awaits, the spirit remains,
Through loved ones, the legacy sustains.

When all is said and all is done,
In this life's lottery, a prize well won.
Love of friends and family stays,
And of the ONE who keeps the tally always.

Rest in Peace and Grace,
Your legacy time will not erase.
Grateful are we that paths did cross,
In this life of qualm and chance.

The doors of heaven open wide,
As ancient verses do confide.
For warriors who embrace the dance,
To face the battle thrust by chance.

32

Tribute to a True Original

A force of nature, bold and free,
Lived life on his own decree.
Said what was meant, meant what was said,
A fearless spirit, far ahead.

A proud son of Sri Lanka,
Made a mark in Canada.
Professional zeal became lore,
And stories live on forevermore.

Met him decades long ago,
In halls where laughter still echoes.
Young and spirited, full of grace,
Bringing warmth to every space.

Blended philosophy with healing art,
Engaged in dialogue, spoke from the heart.
Steadfast courage, conviction displayed,
In discourse and debate, never swayed.

Humor sparkled, joy abound,
Laughter a melody that knew no bounds.
In every room, a spirit shone bright,
Turning even the mundane into light.

A life well lived, a tale so grand,
With wit and wisdom, close at hand.
Not only would he charm and teach,
But through logic, cast a reach.

His life was a classic,
As was his funny magic.
Not only could he pull a rabbit,
But cast a spell too with his logic.

One facet that made him tall,
Was his fearless nature above all.
Ethically sound, kind in ways,
Uncompromising in values, as always.

A spirit devout, serene and wise,
Faith a beacon, a guiding light.
Sought wisdom with a tender heart,
By living life as a mindful art.

Love and memory will endure,
In the hearts that keep them sure.
Eternity calls, yet here remains,
A legacy that won't fade.

33

A Dear Colleague
In Memoriam

*DW was a force
And lived life as she chose
She meant what she said
And said what she meant*

*She was a strong woman
Who navigated life on her terms
Honesty was her guiding star
In every promise, near and far*

Her promises kept through storm and strife
A testimony to a selfless life
She could do this with aplomb
With spouse's abiding love and calm

Feared but admired with class
A born leader she was
She got the entrusted jobs done
Even if raised the ire of some

With a steady hand and healing art
She mended the wounds of troubled hearts
A physician who ministered many with care
And showed them their way out of despair

Her service to the military
Is a testament to her bravery
Her uniform, a shield of grace
A heart of gold within its space

When all is said and all is done
In the DW lottery we have certainly all won
Colleague ! You do have our love and loyalty
And of the ONE above who keeps the tally

May you rest in grace and peace
As your legacy will never cease
We are glad that our paths did cross
In this life of scruple and chance

E

Rearview Reverie

34

Ode to the Medical School Class of 1964

1964 was that magical year
When we all banded together.
Some came from the districts, others city,
Strangers we were, but part of one fraternity.

To college we came, with promise and hopes,
Innocent we were, and knew no ropes.
Our pockets jingled, but only with pennies,
And got by we did, on meager mercies.

Boys and girls were equal, but quite separate,
Too timid to connect, even if desperate.
Here we are now, together wondering,
If wasting those years, was not due to dithering.

Anatomy was taught by professors stern,
Not much interest, did either one earn.
While one counted, our body bones tally,
The other terrified us, willy and nilly.

A teacher obsessed about tissues and sections,
Another snooped into sewers and smelly trenches.
These subjects we passed when finally tested,
Relieved we were, but analy fixated.

One lectured about science of forensics,
With peculiar habits and strange semantics.
Another specialized in bowels and motions,
To the toilets we ran, with his kaolin potions.

One professor rambled, on and on about pathology,
Sounded it did, more like bunkumology.
Then came equations, so precise and grand,
To wake us up, from a slumber on command.

One mused about days, at halls so fine,
And regaled us with tales, some less than divine.
Another had but a roving eye,
Out of luck you were, if you were a guy.

OBGYN was taught by one strict, and other bright,
One was charming, the other too forthright.
One inspired, and the other demanded,
I think you know which one we respected.

A mentor taught bedside with surgical insights,
With questions that gave us some frights.
Enquired he did, about sizes and dimensions,
Of parts that you know, we can't even mention!

Against all odds, we made it to graduation,
Missing sadly though, the glory of convocation.
We all then parted, into many different ways,
To make a difference, in so many ways.

Many went abroad, and some remained,
All worked hard, and success attained.
Foreign lands or homeland, it did not matter,
As all did well, despite the scatter.

The '64 batch stands at crossroads today,
Making sense of life, as it is today.
Wealth to our name is a miracle we say,
As so little we came with, back in the day.

True riches but now are family and friends,
And bonds we fostered in the age of innocence.
When all is said, and all is done,
In the lottery of life, we have certainly all won.

Let's raise our glasses to '64 today,
And celebrate our success on Zoom today.
Let's toast our friendship in virtual space,
And defy the damn virus that's rigged our space.

We wish you all the best of health,
Peace of mind, and enough of wealth.
We wish you fun and happiness galore,
And finally heaven, what could we wish more!

35

Ode to a Caring Friend!

Thought it is a good day today
To thank our man of the day.
He is kind and caring of us all,
As we hunker down within our walls.

He sends us missives
To advise of our finances
And enquires of our children
Like they are his children.

He tells us how to socially distance
By bridging with love the physical distance.
And now that he has us all on the Zoom,
We'll toast him tomorrow for being our boon.

36

Ode to a classmate
An Intrepid Spirit!

First met we did in 1964,
While others knew since years before.
Now as then, remains the chum,
Fearless to the core, an uncut gem.

Raised in a hard working family,
With values of decency and honesty.
Believing in simple plain living,
Coupled with dignity and high thinking.

A natural leader in college days,
Planning this or that with spades.
Behind the scenes, pulling the strings,
Shaping events and guiding things.

Led journeys across the Indian land,
Both North and South, the trips so grand.
Etched in memory, those days remain,
Reminders of youth, our golden age.

Often came college days and parodies,
Kishore Kumar nights and melodies.
The batch of sixty four stood apart,
Inspired by vision, guided by heart.

Challenges he faces in recent days,
Perilously frail, yet strength conveys.
Rising like a Phoenix from painful blues,
Enduring struggles, yet always pushing through.

A comeback force from days gone by,
Bringing together, keeping our ties.
Still planning, dreaming, full of zest,
While others struggle to keep abreast.

Thank you friend for uniting us all,
For spirit strong and standing tall.
An hour to relive the past so bright,
To capture the magic, to share the light.

Let's raise our glasses high today:

For a long life and a healthy one,
For a good love and a cherished one.
For a quick passage and a painless one,
For a good drink and then another one!

37

Happy Mother's Day!

To all mothers today
We bow our heads in praise
You have given us your all
And made our children stand tall
Your sacrifices along the way
Have held our ships from sway
Winter, spring or fall
Splendidly you've served us all
A heartfelt thank you this Sunday
Without your anchor, adrift we are today !

Happy Mothers Day !

38

A World Within me?

Born in Hyderabad's sunlit grace,
To Tamil roots, a southern trace.
In India's heart, I found my start,
Among rich faiths and minds so smart.

Hindus, Muslims, Christians too,
A rainbow of every shade and hue.
Little Flower School shaped my mind,
Where Catholic brothers were gentle, kind.

They taught us all to live as One,
Though different threads, the same cloth spun.
Eid and Christmas lit the skies,
As Diwali danced before our eyes.

Vaisakhi sang in vibrant cheer,
Each festival held bright and dear.
Jana Gana Mana we would sing,
Proud children of Bharat, full of spring.

Then off to England, I did roam,
Yet Hyderabad remained in my bone.
I learned the tea, the rain, the prose,
But my wife kept the sari, with my rose.

Then came Canada, a northern call,
Snowflakes whispering through the fall.
We stirred in maple, warm and sweet,
With spice from home it felt complete.

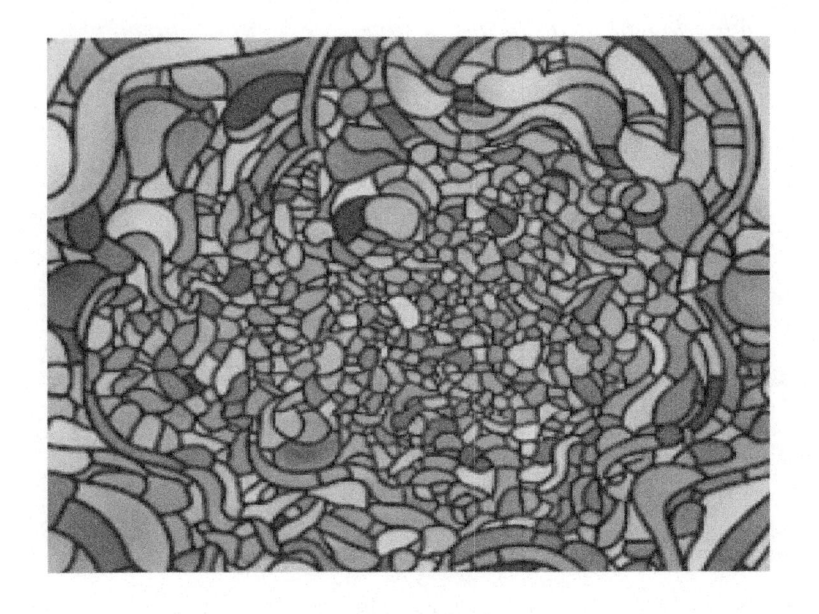

An Indo-Canadian, now my name,
Yet both within me burned the same.
Like rivers meeting at the sea,
Each tide bringing something new to me.

Hyderabad, still beats at my core,
A mystic tale, an ancient lore.
The U.S., Bermuda joined the stream,
And Kiwi lands danced through my dream.

Each place a note in my soul's song,
Each right, each root, where I belong.
I often pause and ask again,
With so much blended, who remains?

A fusion soul of shade and light,
Of mango sun and snowflake white.
A world citizen, I've come to be,
Wearing flags like garments to me.

And now I sing that deeper hymn,
Where Tagore's vision softly swims:
A world unbroken, whole and free,
Where minds awake in unity.

So who am I? I am the sound,
Of many lands in one heart bound.
And when my colours all align,
I become this soul by grand design.

39

Ten Shades of Prose
The G10 Book Club

An email sent without much flair,
Bound ten of us from who knows where.
We hadn't met, nor thought to find,
A kinship forged through books and mind.

At first, the mix was strange and wide,
Doctors, bankers, journalists, side by side.
A lawyer's voice, a CEO's nuance,
Each brought his spark, with a skillful dance.

Of race and color, we were a blend,
With wit and warmth that knew no end.
Though views would clash and ideas compete,
With open hearts, all minds would meet.

We read through thrillers, fiction, and verse,
Modern writers and bygone story tellers.
Each genre found its space and grace,
Each author left a thoughtful trace.

But books alone don't tell the tale,
They're sails we raise to catch the gale.
For through the words, what we became,
Were friends beyond the badge or name.

This club, though cut from printed cloth,
Now beats and breathes with human heart.
Through every page and earnest look,
We've bound our truths beyond the book.

We're G10 now, in jest and pride,
Ten minds that think, ten souls that guide.
Each voice a lens, each thought a key,
Unlocking the truths conjointly by decree.

By knowledge, we have become aware,
That wisdom cuts through dark despair.
He who reads with heart and grace,
Finds True Self, the Bhagavad Gita says.

F

Serving in Silence

40

Ode to Public Service
An Appreciation

The tribunal class of two thousand and twenty
Age and experience in such bounty
Gun shy maybe of newtech learning
But bracing to link and even zooming !

Covid has set a new tone
Hearings now on phone
We do have to atone
For adjudicating in repose !

Separated though by social distance
Grown we have in virtual confidence
Defied we have the Covid scare
And heard all appeals fair and square

To the tribunal staff and leaders we say
Shepherded you have with courage and flair
When all is said and alls done
Thank you all for a job well done

Happy Holidays to you and Family
Think positive and test always negative
Let's say good bye to the year gone by
And welcome the new year with new hope and joy

41

Ode to a Tireless Advocate
A Voice for the Voiceless

A chapter closes, a journey ends,
As a steadfast leader leaves dear friends.
With purpose, heart, and vision bright,
She stood for justice, fought with might.

With confidence, both firm and kind,
A steady voice, a thoughtful mind.
In every challenge, she took her stand,
Upholding rights with guiding hand.

For those unheard, she lent her voice,
Granting them dignity, empowering choice.
Through values deep, she led the way,
Ensuring justice would never stray.

Her words—measured, fair, and wise,
With steady hands and clear eyes.
Never one to wound or slight,
Yet standing firm with quiet might.

Resilient through the hardest fight,
Through trials dark, she held tight.
No power swayed, no fear could bend,
Her will to lead, to see things mend.

She championed rights for all to share,
No voice too small, no cause unfair.
For every culture, race, and creed,
She stood for equity, word and deed.

In halls of power, where deals are spun,
She smiled and listened but got things done.
With wisdom deep and duty true,
She built a team with vision new.

Now the time has come—no stress, no fuss,
We thank you for guiding us!
Your noble work will long remain,
As you step back—but not in vain.

Now you're free to take a break,
No meetings, no calls, no memos to make.
With family near, you'll laugh and sing,
Embracing the joys that new days bring!

G

Home is a Feeling

42

Personal Reflection
If Truth be Told !

Three score and fifteen
Much ado about nothing

Why the soiree today
For coasting to this day
The miles clocked away
And time ebbed away

Not much to write or rave
Footprints blown away
Unring the bell if I may
Roll back the clock to repay

What does matter today
Chime nor time of day
Friendships forged my way
carved in stone to stay

Thank you for your amity
In service of my levity
No lament of unfilled endings
Life's yet full of rich new beginnings

The centerpiece of this life
Beyond years of seventy five
My Love of Family and Glorious Pride
The summit of a prosaic life

43

A Word of Thanks
To my Hometown

From Hyderabad I am
The city of forts and dams
Where the culture of north
Mingles with the south
Where pearls are strung
And church bells rung
Where tongues many spoken
And barriers of religion broken

Where the muezzin call
Echoes through temple halls
Where bridges are built
And friendships forged and sealed
I am who I am
As from Hyderabad I am !

44

Echoes of Generations
A Family Legacy

As we bid farewell with hearts sincere,
We gather in remembrance, year by year.
A time to cherish, to reflect, to see,
The bonds that hold our legacy.

It all began with roots so deep,
A journey taken, a promise to keep.
Through trials faced and battles won,
A guiding light, like the rising sun.

Through changing times, through toil and care,
Families grew with love to share.
Lessons passed through every age,
A story written on history's page.

Children raised with strength and grace,
Navigating life at their own pace.
With wisdom, courage, and hearts so wide,
They stood together, side by side.

New bonds formed, new lives entwined,
A growing tree, deeply aligned.
With every branch, with every name,
A future built, a lasting flame.

Through every era, through joy and strife,
They shaped the path of love and life.

45

The Cost of Desire
Emmanuel's Lament

Emmanuel sends a musing,
Of Man's eternal recycling.
The blue boxes hold the elements,
The remnants of our sediments.

We are robbing nature,
Of God given treasure.
We take what is not ours,
And beg no mercy from our forebears.

The planet we were to cherish,
We let it fade, we let it perish.
The sunlight meant to warm and flower,
We stain with greed and choke with power.

The holy rain Gods upon us pour,
No longer pure, comes down impure.
We've turned the sweet to bitter spoil,
And poisoned earth with thoughtless toil.

Emmanuel reminds we daily consume,
The very poisons we daily exhume.
The blue box stands, a quiet metaphor,
For caskets waiting for us to enter.

When desire enslaves the wandering mind,
Gita says, anger follows, cruel and blind,
Delusion clouds, all wisdom lost,
Man ruins himself, and pays the cost.

46

A Good Walk, After All!

Sneered I did at this game,
Until I was close to a cane.
"A good walk spoiled," said Twain,
Not worthy of the thinking brain.

Then I heard it's more than a game,
A skill worth learning, even if lame.
Humility it teaches you for sure,
That we are vulnerable evermore.

A great drive sends you to paradise,
A bad swing lands in bunker vice.
Hell or high water, you return to the course,
For that one sweet putt, the opposite force.

Don't dwell upon the hole you played,
Its highs and lows will surely fade.
The next one waits, fresh hope in sight,
Like life, a chance, to set things right.

Friends I have made on every walk,
Hard truths shared in every talk.
Tiger Woods I'm not, that's for sure,
And vanity's not part of my score.

A golfer I am, that's true lore,
Mostly over par, yet I ask for more.
Glad I picked up the iron club,
Silently bitten by this blissful bug.

Strive your best, yet hold no claim,
Joy and loss, are just the same.
The mystery ride of the golf drive,
Is Karma, our soul's only true guide.

Notes and Reflections

Notes and Reflections

Notes and Reflections

Notes and Reflections

Notes and Reflections

Notes and Reflections

Notes and Reflections

Notes and Reflections

Made in United States
North Haven, CT
03 August 2025